JAY-JAY
THE SUPERSONIC BUS

UNIVERSITY OF CHICHESTER

D1471411

WS 2400720 X

Sue Wickstead

Published in 2014 by Sue Wickstead
ISBN: 978-0-9930737-0-0

Written by Sue Wickstead
Illustration by Artful Doodlers
Layout design by Claire Shaw

© Sue Wickstead 2014
All rights reserved. No part of this publication may be reproduced in any form.

Printed in Great Britain by The Holywell Press Ltd.

JAY-JAY
THE SUPERSONIC BUS

SUE WICKSTEAD

For Tom and Elly.
Without whom I would never have met Jay-Jay.

For Alex
Who was in the book, you know!

"This one! This is the bus we want!"

It had been a while since Jay-Jay had felt wanted. He remembered how he had once been just an ordinary bus taking passengers on their many journeys. JJK 261 Route B.

More recently, Jay-Jay had begun to feel tired and old; he might break down, splutter to a halt, or just not start properly in the morning. He had been sent to the dreary, dirty scrap yard where all the old buses were sent to end their days. This made him feel useless and unwanted. He prepared himself to stand alone and miserable gathering dust, broken down for parts, or worst of all left to rust.

The only thing that happened in the last
few weeks had been a visit from some cheeky
children who had come along to play on him.
They had climbed inside and pretended to be bus
drivers. They had been a little rough and boisterous
as they played; running noisily up and down the
stairs, but Jay-Jay hadn't minded too much because
he was enjoying their adventure too! He was glad of
their company and knew they were just using their
imagination.

The angry man in the breaker's yard didn't think
so and had chased them away with shouts of,
"Too dangerous! It's not safe!"

"Dangerous?" Jay-Jay had thought to himself. "Not
safe? Why am I not safe?" The words had hurt him and
sadly Jay-Jay had resigned himself to being left alone,
with only the spiders spinning webs for company.

But today was different. He had watched as three people had arrived at the scrap yard. They had looked around at the buses in the yard. He was worried that maybe they had come to take a few of his pieces, to take him apart and break him up, but no!

They seemed to be muttering to the man in the yard about taking all of him.

"What do they want me for?" Jay-Jay wondered.

He listened curiously, trying to understand what was going on. The men were talking about children and play. He wondered if he was in trouble following his boisterous visitors. The conversation sounded interesting and Jay-Jay couldn't help but feel a little excited!

There was a moment's pause and Jay-Jay held his breath, watching as the people talked amongst themselves checking through their paperwork. Then with a shake of a hand, a deal was done. Jay-Jay breathed a sigh of relief.

SCRAP
YARD

NOT IN
SERVICE

SOLD

JJK 261

"I wonder where I am off to?"
he thought to himself "I hope
it is better than this!"

One of the men climbed
aboard and started the
engine. It had been a
while, so it took a few
spluttering attempts
before Jay-Jay eventually
grumbled into action.

Jay-Jay felt nervous and excited. He had no idea where he was
going but felt safe in the hands of the driver who steered him
carefully out of the scrap yard and onto the busy roads. He made
his way hesitantly, his joints creaking a little after being sat still
for so long.

He could feel his engine warming up. Purring loudly, he drove along the dusty roads, taking in the sights and sounds.

It had been so long since he had been taken out for a drive and it was a lovely feeling to be moving again, with the feel of warm diesel racing through his pipes and the breeze through his radiator. He felt alive and excited!

"This is great!" beamed Jay-Jay to himself.

After some time Jay-Jay eventually came to a shuddering halt,
he looked up at the important looking buildings and huge garage
doors in front of him.

"What is this place?" wondered Jay-Jay.

All was revealed as the doors noisily began
to open. Lorries! Aeroplanes!
"This must be an airport!"

Jay-Jay had seen aeroplanes before but not up close like this. They had always seemed so small when flying over him up high in the sky, but here on the ground they towered over him on their huge wheels with their wings spread out wide.

"What am I doing here?" he thought.

He heard a voice of one of the mechanics echo across the hangar.

"Look!" he called. "Here is our magic bus!"

"Magic bus?" wondered Jay-Jay curiously. "Surely they can't be talking about me?"

The word 'magic' went through Jay-Jay's mind. "What's so magic about me?"

The men were talking about children and play once again, of new houses and school holidays. They said that the children would need somewhere safe to play and that he was going to help out.

Here in the hangar where the aeroplanes were repaired, he was going to be turned into a 'Playbus' full of all the exciting things to help the children play; a bus full of imagination! He would drive to the children visiting them wherever they were, he would light up their lives with colour and happiness.

"Wow!" thought Jay-Jay, "I like children, and I love to play!"

Jay-Jay was so excited he would be getting a new life and a new purpose. He would not have to be broken up for scrap, and to Jay-Jay this was the magic part!

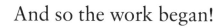

And so the work began!

The first task was to take out all the seats from inside the bus, both upstairs and downstairs.

"This is strange!" thought Jay-Jay. "Where will the children sit?"

But this was the exciting part! The children didn't need to sit down; he wouldn't need to drive them around. There were regular buses for that. Their journeys would be filled with play; their journeys would be in their imagination!

The next few weeks saw Jay-Jay transformed into a bright colourful masterpiece! He was cleaned inside and given a new, bright and sparkly, coat of paint.

Upstairs, they put in a carpet area. Cupboards were built and stuffed full to the brim with exciting new toys for the children to choose to play with.

Here were toys and games, bricks for building, a train track, a dolls house, and lots of soft toys.

There were books to read and puzzles to put together.

Best of all, there was a little home corner with tea sets and crockery. The cupboard there was full of fancy-dress clothes and hats to dress up in, everything to make the home cosy and warm.

Downstairs they made an area where children could paint, draw and make models with glue. Here they could do all the messy creative things. There was play dough to squash, roll out and mould. There was even a sandpit too!

"This looks fun!" thought Jay-Jay excitedly.

Now all they needed was to make his outside just as bright and colourful too, this would attract the attention of the children and get them running to come and explore!

Onto the outside a slide could be fitted where the children would climb up and race down the bonnet of the bus.

"They'll love this!" thought Jay-Jay.

Jay-Jay was painted in bright bold colours; it had pictures of children with smiling happy faces. He was especially pleased that they had painted an aeroplane along both of his sides.

With his colourful new coat Jay-Jay raced happily along the road beside the runway. He watched as the aeroplanes roared along lifting up into the sky and he wondered where they were off to.

He would race along the road beside them, but no matter how fast he drove and no matter how hard he tried to use the speed bumps to help him jump up high and fly, he stayed firmly on the ground.

"If only they had fitted me with wings," sighed Jay-Jay. "Oh well! I suppose with all my precious cargo of new toys I might be safer on the ground."

But now most importantly, he was given a new name for his new start!

Of course, Jay-Jay was only his registration number. His name was painted brightly along his sides; 'Supersonic'.

"I like my new name!" thought Jay-Jay and he knew he would fly in the imagination of his many new friends. He might not actually be able to fly but he knew it would be a great reminder of his airport days and of the fun he had chasing the planes along the runway.

After many weeks of work Jay-Jay the 'Supersonic' bus, was ready to meet the children.

He felt a little sad to be leaving the airport, but he was also very excited to be getting a new life and a new start.

When he saw all the smiling faces of the children who came out to meet him he felt proud and happy to be helping out and he knew what an important job it was.

He loved how the children laughed and played, both inside and outside the bus. It made him feel tingly inside. Wherever he went the children would run excitedly to see their 'Playbus' and they loved him.

The children loved to paint and Jay-Jay the Supersonic bus didn't mind getting a few splashes over him or sand in his cracks.

The children especially loved the slide. They loved to climb up onto the bus bonnet and imagine they were driving. It reminded him of the children in the dirty dusty scrap yard all those months ago and with a warm shiver he felt how lucky he was to have escaped being broken up into pieces.

Noisily or quietly, it didn't matter which, he was just happy that they were having fun and so was he.

But then as summer started to come to an end there was talk of school and the children's numbers began to fall.

"What is going to happen to me now?" he wondered.

"Will I be sent back to the scrap yard? I hope not!"

He would be sad of course if he had to go back to the dirty dusty scrap yard. But no matter what, this most certainly had been a great adventure and he had made so many new friends! The children had loved him and he had given them a fun and exciting place to play.

Most of all he had felt loved and wanted again.

Then suddenly, a very important message arrived, just in time.

It was a message from The Queen!

He had been invited to Buckingham Palace where he was going to receive a special award for all of his hard work.

"Wow!" Jay-Jay was so surprised! "Me?" he thought, "Can this really be true or just a dream?"

Surely it was he who should say thank you for being rescued and being able to meet so many children. He felt so pleased when he was given his bright sparkly medal; he beamed proudly in the sunlight.

What a great honour!

The news of the award spread around town and many visitors came to see what all the fuss was about.

They wanted to see the now famous 'Jay-Jay the Supersonic Bus'.

With the older children back at school Jay-Jay was to be given a new adventure providing a playgroup for the smaller children.

The older children would never forget the fun they had thanks to Jay-Jay or the adventures that he gave them, nor would he forget them, but for now it was time for a new adventure to begin.